There's a giant in the woods at the Lost Gardens of Heligan! He found his way there by travelling round the gardens. On his way, he came across all kinds of amazing things, including a pong, a putto, a scarecrow, some stripey buzzers, a hot seat and some spooks! You can see all the places he visited and follow his adventures, until at last you meet him in the spot he likes best of all. Don't forget to show him a friendly face; he likes that better than anything!

To find out more about where the giant lives now, visit www.heligan.com

For all the friendly faces at Heligan! *SH*

For my father, with love. *KP*

# The Giant

First published in the United Kingdom in 2006 by
The Clucket Press
220 Hill Lane
Southampton
Hants
SO15 7NR
www.tattybogle.com

Paperback  isbn 13:  978-0-9549256-2-8

3579108642

Layout and setting by Niall Horn
Printed in the United Kingdom by BORCOMBE SP, Romsey, Hampshire.

# THE GIANT

By

Sandra Horn          Karen Popham

The Clucket Press

Once, the giant lived in a tin mine.
He liked to chat to the miners when they had their crib.
He liked their friendly faces.

One day they said, "They'm closing the mine
d'reckly, boy. We won't be coming here no more."
The giant was sad.
"T'will be some lonesome," he said,
"with no friendly faces. Reckons I'll go too."

After the miners had gone, the giant set off through the shafts.
When he came to a patch of soft earth, he tunnelled upwards.
Suddenly, he was in sunlight! He blinked.
All around, flowers grew, trees blossomed, birds sang.
A man holding a fork was standing close by.

"Oi!" said the man, "What's that gurt lump in me flower bed?
How can I plant me bulbs in that?"
"That ain't no friendly face!" said the giant,
and he ducked back under the ground.

He burrowed along a little way, then put his head out again.
He saw a little tacker fighting with a fish.
"You'd best leave that poor fish alone and get some clothes on
'fore you catches cold, me boy!" said the giant.
The little tacker smiled. "I'm not your boy," he said, "I'm a putto."
"Well, putto that fisho downo!" said the giant, and he laughed.

He laughed so hard, the ground shook.
The putto wobbled. He stopped smiling.
"Go away! You're making an earthquake!" he cried.
"Oops!" said the giant, and he dived back underground.

"That be two of 'em I've upset now," the giant sighed.
He tunnelled a little further and popped up in a big glass box.
It was full of spiky plants with luscious golden fruits!
"Yum!" said the giant.

Then he noticed a powerful pong.
"Yuk!" he said.  Down he went again.

The giant tunnelled away from the pong.
When he put his head out again,
he was surrounded by vegetables!
"Cor!" he said.
A strange man shouted,
"Begone afore I skat 'ee, crow!
Skedaddle! Oppit! Shoo!"
"Hang on a minute, mate!" said the giant,
"Do I look like a crow?"
"You said cor," said the man,
"you must be a crow. Oppit!"

"That's not friendly!" said the giant,
"Down I goes again."

When the giant put his head back out,
he saw rows of baskets set into a wall.
There was a gorgeous smell of honey in the air.
He climbed right out of the ground
and put his thumb in one of the baskets.
He pulled it out covered in golden goo.
He was just going to lick it,
when a crowd of little stripey buzzers flew at him.
They landed all over his head.
"Ping!"
"Ouch!" said the giant, "Don't be teazy!  Leave I be!"
But they wouldn't leave him be,
so he dived underground again, fast.

The next time the giant put his head out, nothing was buzzing.
"That's all right, then," he said.
He saw a little round house on a pole.
He tapped on one of the doors.
A white feathery head peeped out.
The giant clapped his hands.
"Ansome!" he cried.
Frightened birds burst out of the doors and flew up into the air.
The giant called, "Don't go!  I only wants to be your friend!"
But it was too late. They'd all flown away.

The giant sighed and sank beneath the ground.
"I didn't mean to upset 'em," he said.
He tunnelled on a little way.
When he came up again, he saw more birds.
"Dunnee be frightened," he whispered.
They weren't frightened! They were running at him,
clattering their sharp beaks!
"Quack! Peck! Chooky! Peck!" they cackled.
"Ouch! That's not friendly!" said the giant,
and he dived down out of harm's way.

When his nose had stopped throbbing,
the giant climbed out of the ground again.  He was by a little house.
He knelt down and peered in through the window.
He saw a picture on the wall.  Three white faces with big black eyes.
Then the picture moved! A white face turned to look at him.
A black eye winked.
"Spooks!" cried the giant.  "I'm off!"

The giant leaped over a gate and into a sloping field.
The grass was long and soft and sweet.  He chuckled.
He lay down and went roley-poley-poley
all the way to the bottom of the field.
"Whee! Proper Job!" he said, "I haven't done that
since I were a little tacker!"

When he got up, his head was swimmy,
his eyes were blurry, his legs were jelly.
He staggered down a sunken lane,
into a wood.
"I needs a sit-down," he said.

The air in the wood was hazy and smelled of woodsmoke.
In a clearing, the giant saw some big round metal seats.
"Just the right size for I!" he said. He sat down on one –
and jumped straight back up again!
"Ow! Ow! My backside's afire!"

The giant went hopping and howling out of the wood.
He leaped up a steep bank, ran through some jungly
trees and jumped into a cool, deep pond.
"Ooh, aah!" he sighed.
A squirmy fish swam up his nose.
"Oh, yergh!" he cried. "**A-a-ah choo**!"
The fish shot out and swam away.

"There! All I wants is a friend," the giant muttered,
"but everywhere I goes, there's trouble!
Where can I go, where I can't upset nobody
and they can't upset I?"
Soggy and sad, he climbed out of the pond.
"I'll give it one more try," he said.
He tunnelled under a grassy slope.

When the giant put his head out next, he was by a woodland path.
It was cool and shady under the trees.
Nothing was flapping or pecking or squirming.
Nobody shouted, nothing ponged or buzzed or burned.
He began to feel cheerful again.

Soon, he came to a flowery glade.
"Hush!"
Someone was sleeping among the ferns.
She smiled in her sleep as the giant came by.
"Now that's a friendly face!" he whispered.

The giant tunnelled a little way off so as not to disturb her.
At the edge of the wood, he came up through a patch of primroses.
"I'll just bide me time here," he said, "until she wakes up."

THANK YOU to John and Katy Allen, our Cornish experts, Sue Hill and Pete Hill who created the Giant and allowed us to tell his story, Candy Smit and the Heligan team, Barry Lockyer, Jenny Lorimer, Christopher Popham and Ellie Popham, for your invaluable help, advice and support in the making of this book.

Also by Sandra Horn and Karen Popham:

The Mud Maid is a magical tale of how the Gardens came to be lost and found and restored to life and beauty once again.

*This is a beautiful, haunting picture book. The lyrical text is perfectly complemented by the luminous pictures...* Armadillo

*A story of regeneration which will appeal to all ages. Strange and beautiful pictures accompany this lyrical tale of the Mud Maid who inhabits an idyllic garden...* The Bookseller

*..moving and original...* The Independent Online

*..this beautiful story with its evocative illustrations...* The School Librarian

The Mud Maid is also published by The Clucket Press.

Hardcover isbn 13:  978-0-9549256-1-1
Paperback  isbn 13:  978-0-9549256-0-4

# Also from the Clucket Press:

*A story by Sandra Horn illustrated by Mervyn Hathaway - set in Furzey Gardens in the New Forest*

Some of the oak trees in Furzey Gardens are a hundred years old or more. Their tall green crowns reach up towards the sky. On gusty days, the leaves whisper stories told by the wind. The oldest oak of all is hidden away. It bears no green leaves or acorns now, but it too has a story.

Paperback  isbn 13:  978-0-9549256-5-9

*And also: a new way to enjoy an old friend!*

A cd audiobook of the well-loved story read by the author complemented by the enchanting songs written by Ruth Kenward for Tattybogle the Musical. For samples of the music, go to www.starshine.co.uk.

isbn 13;  978-0-9549256-4-2

*A favourite story by Sandra Horn, illustrated by Esther Connon, now available again!*

The cat wants a dish of cream, the rat would like a whole blue cheese. Gran needs a silken pillow for her poor old head and the boy just wishes for a silver penny. Then one dark night, they look up and see a round white moon. They each think their dream has come true…

Paperback isbn 13:  978-0-9549256-6-6